THIS BOOK BELONGS TO...

Name:

Favourite player:

2024/25

My Predictions	Actual

The Foxes' final position:

The Foxes' top scorer:

Premier League winners:

Premier League top scorer:

FA Cup winners:

EFL Cup winners:

Contributors: Andy Greeves, Peter Rogers

A TWOCAN PUBLICATION

©2024. Published by twocan under licence from Leicester City Football Club.
Every effort has been made to ensure the accuracy of information within this publication but the publishers cannot be held responsible for any errors or omissions. Views expressed are those of the authors and do not necessarily represent those of the publishers or the football club. All rights reserved.

978-1-916755-13-0

PICTURE CREDITS:
Alamy, Leicester City FC, Plumb Images.

CONTENTS

Premier League Squad 24/25	06
Footy Drills - Fitness First	22
Ricardo Pereira Poster	23
Meet Your Rivals	24
LCFC Women	28
LCFC Women Squad 24/25	30
Wordsearch	36
Conor Coady Poster	37
Big Match - Goals	38
Jutta Rantala Poster	39
Danger Men	40
Young Player of the Season	44
Footy Drills - Attack Attack	46
Abdul Fatawu Poster	47
Harry Winks Poster	48
Snap Shot	49
Women's Player of the Season	50
Women's Goal of the Season	51
Fact or Fib?	52
Footy Drills - Shot Stopping	54
Wilfred Ndidi Poster	55
Goal of the Season	56
Big Match - Appearances	58
Janina Leitzig Poster	59
Jamie Vardy Poster	60
Complete the Badge	61
Answers	62

LCFC MEN SQUAD 24/25

DANNY WARD — **1**

POSITION: Goalkeeper   COUNTRY: Wales   DOB: 22/06/1993

Ward has been at the Club since 2018, having previously played for Liverpool, and regularly stars for Wales, making his third tournament appearance during the 2022 FIFA World Cup. The shot-stopper featured twice in City's run to lifting the Emirates FA Cup in 2021, since playing in both the Premier League and UEFA Europa League.

JAMES JUSTIN — 2

POSITION: Defender   COUNTRY: England   DOB: 23/02/1998

The full-back, who can play on either flank, arrived from Luton Town in 2019, becoming a key member of Leicester's squad and also earning a senior England cap in 2022. Justin's ability and experience proved to be useful in gaining promotion from the Sky Bet Championship and his stunning strike at Cardiff City won the Club's Goal of the Season award.

WOUT FAES — 3

POSITION: Defender   COUNTRY: Belgium   DOB: 03/04/1998

Belgian centre-back Faes brought experience at both club and international level after joining in 2022, culminating in automatic promotion back to the Premier League for 2024/25. Displaying his dedicated displays in defence, he was a key cog in the Club's resurgence, playing 43 times in the Sky Bet Championship, scoring away at both Blackburn Rovers and Leeds United respectively.

LCFC MEN SQUAD 24/25

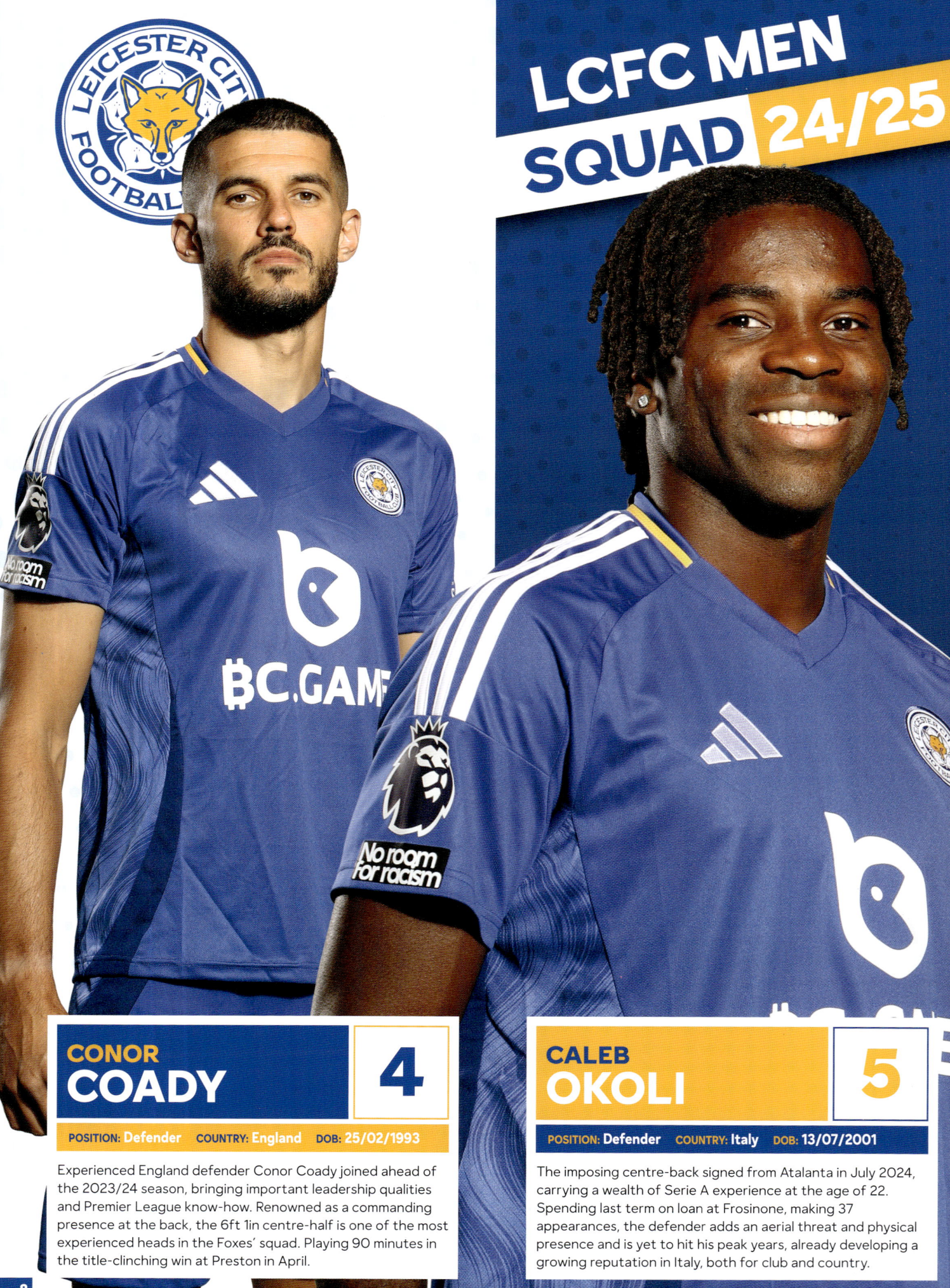

CONOR COADY — 4
POSITION: Defender **COUNTRY:** England **DOB:** 25/02/1993

Experienced England defender Conor Coady joined ahead of the 2023/24 season, bringing important leadership qualities and Premier League know-how. Renowned as a commanding presence at the back, the 6ft 1in centre-half is one of the most experienced heads in the Foxes' squad. Playing 90 minutes in the title-clinching win at Preston in April.

CALEB OKOLI — 5
POSITION: Defender **COUNTRY:** Italy **DOB:** 13/07/2001

The imposing centre-back signed from Atalanta in July 2024, carrying a wealth of Serie A experience at the age of 22. Spending last term on loan at Frosinone, making 37 appearances, the defender adds an aerial threat and physical presence and is yet to hit his peak years, already developing a growing reputation in Italy, both for club and country.

WILFRED NDIDI

6

POSITION: Midfielder COUNTRY: Nigeria DOB: 16/12/1996

A tall and combative central midfielder with plenty of quality, the Nigeria international is now one of the Club's longest serving players having signed from KRC Genk in January 2017. The Emirates FA Cup winner contributed four goals and five assists to the Sky Bet Championship title-winning campaign before agreeing a new three-year deal in the summer of 2024.

ABDUL FATAWU

7

POSITION: Forward COUNTRY: Ghana DOB: 08/03/2004

The Ghana international established himself as a fans' favourite on Filbert Way during an initial loan spell in 2023/24, before making the move permanent by signing a five-year contract. The first hat-trick of his senior career, in the 5-0 rout of Southampton, outlined his growing talent and moved City one step closer to the promotion which was confirmed six days later.

LCFC MEN SQUAD 24/25

HARRY WINKS — 8
POSITION: Midfielder **COUNTRY:** England **DOB:** 02/01/1996

Signing from Tottenham Hotspur last summer, the Englishman quickly demonstrated his ability to play as a deep-lying playmaker. A talented passer and controller of the tempo, his qualities came to fore in the Sky Bet Championship title-winning season, becoming a crucial figure during 2023/24. Featuring in all-but one of City's league fixtures, Winks' influence on becoming second-tier champions cannot be understated.

JAMIE VARDY — 9
POSITION: Forward **COUNTRY:** England **DOB:** 11/01/1987

Vardy once again showed his immense value in 2023/24, top scoring with 20 goals to fire the Foxes to the Championship title. He signed a new one-year deal ahead of Leicester's Premier League return and is now the Club's third top goalscorer of all time. City's No.9 is also close to climbing into the top three of the Club's all-time appearances charts.

LCFC MEN SQUAD 24/25

STEPHY MAVIDIDI — 10

POSITION: Forward **COUNTRY:** England **DOB:** 31/05/1998

Attacking talent Mavididi joined in the summer of 2023 from French Ligue 1 side Montpellier and has become a significant figure in the Foxes' XI, contributing to Sky Bet Championship promotion. Nine goals by New Year's Day earned the winger the league's December Player of the Month award. Mavididi featured in all 46 league fixtures, scoring 12 times and assisting six further goals.

BILAL EL KHANNOUSS — 11

POSITION: Midfielder **COUNTRY:** Morocco **DOB:** 10/05/2004

Born in Belgium, the talented attacker penned a four-year deal with the Foxes in late August 2024, before making his Premier League debut as a substitute during the home clash with Aston Villa two days later. The Former Genk star recently earned international honours, helping Morocco to a bronze medal at the Paris 2024 Olympics, having also played in the 2022 FIFA World Cup.

BOBBY DE CORDOVA-REID — 14

POSITION: Forward **COUNTRY:** Jamaica **DOB:** 02/02/1993

The Bristolian joined on a three-year contract after five years at Fulham, where he made a significant impact, twice winning promotion to the top flight, reaching a double century of games for the Whites. The skilful attacker, who primarily operates from either flank or as an inside forward, plays internationally for Jamaica, featuring in Copa América this summer.

VICTOR KRISTIANSEN — 16

POSITION: Defender **COUNTRY:** Denmark **DOB:** 16/12/2002

Denmark international Kristiansen joined City in January 2023 and has just completed a season-long loan at Bologna, earning a spot in the UEFA Champions League with a fifth-place Serie A finish, a competition he previously featured in for hometown club FC Copenhagen. His Foxes debut at Walsall was a success, before impressing on his Premier League bow - a 4-2 win at Aston Villa.

HAMZA CHOUDHURY — 17

POSITION: Midfielder **COUNTRY:** England **DOB:** 01/10/1997

At Leicester since 2005, making over a century of appearances for the Foxes, Choudhury appeared in the Club's Emirates FA Cup triumph and has since captained the Club on several occasions. Utilised as an inverted full-back last term, a heroic defensive display against West Bromwich Albion helped the Foxes secure a crucial victory on the way to being crowned Sky Bet Championship champions.

LCFC MEN SQUAD 24/25

JORDAN AYEW — 18
POSITION: Forward **COUNTRY:** Ghana **DOB:** 11/09/1991

An experienced striker, Marseille-born Ayew signed from Crystal Palace on a two-year-deal in August 2024, debuting for the Foxes against Fulham that month. Previously making 212 appearances for the Eagles in all competitions, following spells with Swansea City and Aston Villa, the 32-year-old has also represented his country at two FIFA World Cups and six Africa Cup of Nations, surpassing 100 caps.

PATSON DAKA — 20
POSITION: Forward **COUNTRY:** Zambia **DOB:** 09/10/1998

Zambia international Daka continues to make his mark for the Foxes, proving a useful weapon in the Sky Bet Championship last term. Four goals in December helped City win all but one game that month, before a brace in the 5-0 victory at Stoke City after returning from AFCON. His LCFC goal tally stood at seven in 20 games across 2023/24.

LCFC MEN SQUAD 24/25

RICARDO PEREIRA — 21
POSITION: Defender **COUNTRY:** Portugal **DOB:** 06/10/1993

Ricardo has established himself as a firm fans' favourite since joining in 2018 and recently lifted the Sky Bet Championship trophy, having captained the side on numerous occasions. A full-back by trade, the Portuguese international was utilised in a central midfield role across 2023/24, contributing three goals and three assists in 39 league appearances, including a Goal of the Season contender at Watford.

OLIVER SKIPP — 22
POSITION: Midfielder **COUNTRY:** England **DOB:** 16/09/2000

Skipp joined from Tottenham Hotspur on a five-year contract in August 2024, making his debut against Fulham that month. At Spurs since the age of five, he progressed through the Academy ranks to make 106 senior appearances. The England youth international was coached by Steve Cooper at Under-17s and Under-18s level, before helping the Under-21s to win the 2023 UEFA European Under-21 Championships.

JANNIK VESTERGAARD — 23
POSITION: Defender **COUNTRY:** Denmark **DOB:** 03/08/1992

Former Southampton centre-back Vestergaard joined the Club in the summer of 2021, becoming a key figure in the title-winning side of 2023/24. The towering 6ft 6in Denmark international was almost an ever-present, making 42 league appearances as Leicester lifted the second-tier trophy, completing more passes than any other player in the division and popping up with two goals.

BOUBAKARY SOUMARÉ — 24
POSITION: Midfielder **COUNTRY:** France **DOB:** 27/02/1999

The Frenchman joined City in July 2021 after lifting the Ligue 1 title with Lille. On loan at Sevilla across 2023/24, the 6ft 2in central midfielder showcased his abilities as a reliable figure in possession, appearing 33 times and played 90 minutes in 15 consecutive matches as Rojiblancos moved clear of relegation danger, also featuring in the UEFA Champions League.

ODSONNE ÉDOUARD — 29

POSITION: Forward **COUNTRY:** France **DOB:** 16/01/1998

The Foxes agreed a deal with Crystal Palace for the loan of striker Édouard on the final day of the summer transfer window. Previously at Paris Saint-Germain as a youngster, before four trophy-laden seasons in Scotland with Celtic, a move to the Premier League with Crystal Palace in 2021 led to eight goals in the 2023/24 campaign, which helped earn a 10th placed finish.

MADS HERMANSEN — 30

POSITION: Goalkeeper **COUNTRY:** Denmark **DOB:** 11/07/2000

Hermansen joined from Brøndby last summer, playing a key role in securing an immediate Premier League return. The Dane featured 44 times in 2023/24, keeping 13 clean sheets, as City sealed the Sky Bet Championship title, leading to Hermansen being named in the EFL Team of the Season, before being called up to the Denmark squad for UEFA EURO 2024.

LCFC MEN SQUAD 24/25

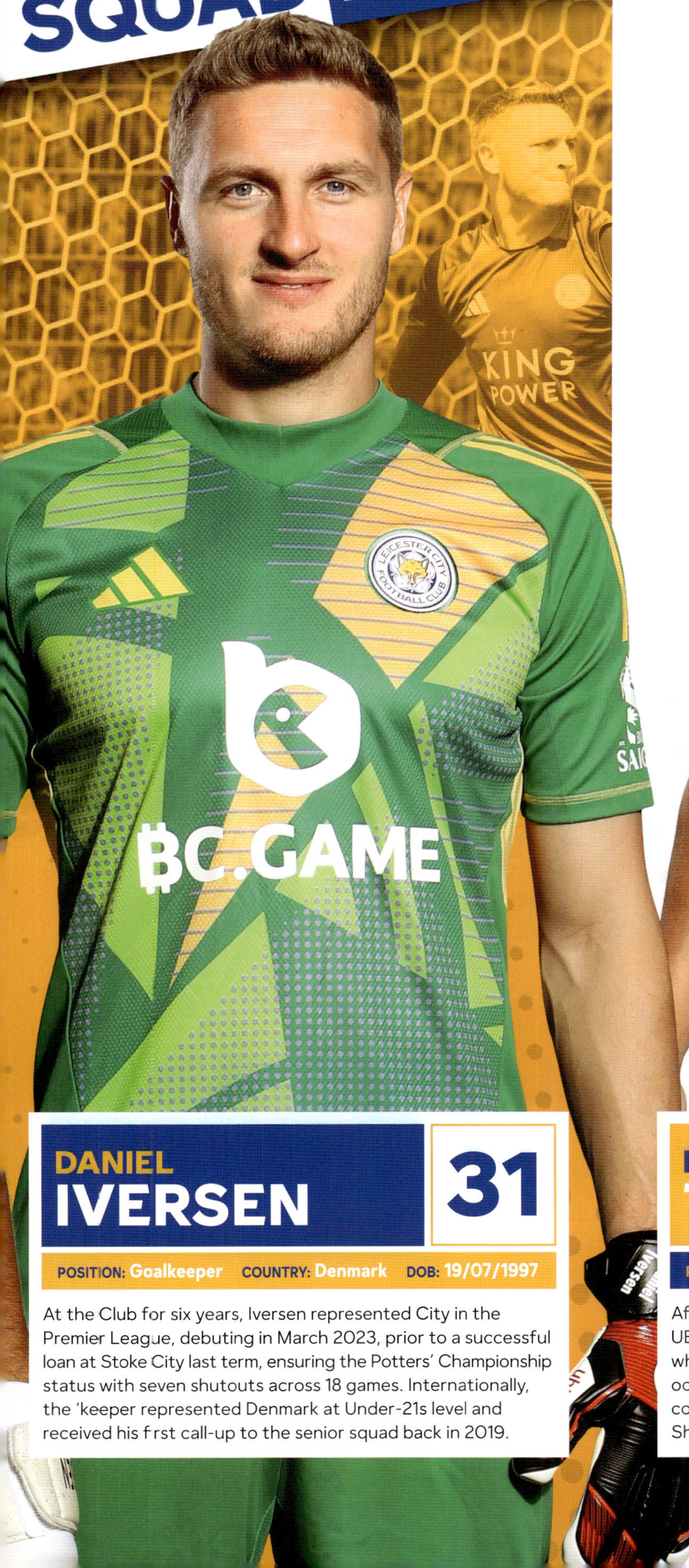

DANIEL IVERSEN — 31
POSITION: Goalkeeper **COUNTRY:** Denmark **DOB:** 19/07/1997

At the Club for six years, Iversen represented City in the Premier League, debuting in March 2023, prior to a successful loan at Stoke City last term, ensuring the Potters' Championship status with seven shutouts across 18 games. Internationally, the 'keeper represented Denmark at Under-21s level and received his first call-up to the senior squad back in 2019.

LUKE THOMAS — 33
POSITION: Defender **COUNTRY:** England **DOB:** 10/06/2001

After lifting the Emirates FA Cup as a 19-year-old in 2021, UEFA U21 EURO champion and Academy graduate Thomas, who has been with the Club since 2008, has shone on many occasions, both in the Premier League and European competitions, continuing his development out on loan at Sheffield United and then Middlesbrough across 2023/24.

LCFC MEN SQUAD 24/25

MICHAEL GOLDING — 34
POSITION: Midfielder **COUNTRY:** England **DOB:** 23/05/2006

An industrious central midfielder, Golding signed a four-year contract in July 2024 having developed his footballing talents at Chelsea, where he made his senior debut six months earlier. The 18-year-old led England into the UEFA European U17 Championships, before playing in the FIFA U17 World Cup. Now an Under-18s international, Golding helped the team lift the 2024 U18 Pinatar Super Cup.

KASEY McATEER — 35
POSITION: Midfielder **COUNTRY:** Republic of Ireland **DOB:** 22/11/2001

With the Club since the age of eight, he made his Leicester debut in 2021 after breaking through the Academy ranks. The versatile midfielder then scored his first senior goals for the Foxes in the Sky Bet Championship title-winning campaign, including both strikes during an away victory at Rotherham United, and also netted in the win that confirmed Leicester as champions.

FACUNDO BUONANOTTE — 40
POSITION: Midfielder **COUNTRY:** Argentina **DOB:** 23/12/2004

Buonanotte signed on a season-long loan from Brighton & Hove Albion in August 2024, adding flair and a goalscoring threat to Leicester's ranks. An Argentina international, the 19-year-old attacker has won two senior caps for his country, while he made 36 appearances for the Seagulls last term, featuring in the Premier League and UEFA Europa League, scoring on four occasions.

JAKUB STOLARCZYK — 41
POSITION: Goalkeeper **COUNTRY:** Poland **DOB:** 19/12/2000

Stolarczyk emerged through the Under-21s to make his senior league debut for the Club in a victory at Huddersfield Town last season and was handed more game time in cup competitions. Six clean sheets in nine appearances across the season was an impressive return for the goalkeeper, who was also between the sticks when City clinched the Sky Bet Championship title.

YOU WILL NEED CONES OR MARKERS, A BALL AND A FRIEND!

SHUTTLE RUNS ARE A GREAT FITNESS TRAINING EXERCISE TO HELP BUILD SPEED, STAMINA, ACCELERATION AND ENDURANCE.

FOOTY DRILLS

FITNESS FIRST

EASY

Set up a line of 6-8 cones 5 metres apart. To begin with, run from the first cone to the second cone and back again. Next, run to the second cone and back again. Continue to do this until you have completed a run to the final cone.

HARD

Now, add a football into the mix! Dribble from the start to the first cone, turn with the ball, pass back to your friend and then sprint back to the start. Your friend should stop the ball at the start where you will gain possession and dribble to the second cone. Repeat this process for each of the cones.

EXPERT

There are many ways you can increase the difficulty level of this drill. Have your friend throw the ball to you as you're running back to the start. You will have to work to bring the ball under control, bring it back to the start and dribble on to the next cone - work on chest traps, thigh traps or traps with the feet.

Adding a football helps players control the ball at top speeds and when the body is tired.

Remember to swap roles with your friend so you both get a chance to work on your fitness!

START

As you improve, try and work faster. Try inventing some of your own ways to make this drill harder?

It's time to get to grips with the Premier League and...

MEET YOUR RIVALS

GARY SHAW, TONY MORLEY & PETER WITHE WITH THE 1982 EUROPEAN CUP

AFC BOURNEMOUTH

GROUND: Vitality Stadium **CAPACITY:** 11,307
MANAGER: Andoni Iraola
NICKNAME: The Cherries
2023/24 LEAGUE POSITION: 12th

DID YOU KNOW:
Bournemouth's Vitality Stadium has the smallest capacity in the Premier League.

ASTON VILLA

GROUND: Villa Park **CAPACITY:** 42,657
MANAGER: Unai Emery **NICKNAME:** The Villans
2023/24 LEAGUE POSITION: 4th

DID YOU KNOW:
Aston Villa will compete in the UEFA Champions League in 2024/25, a trophy they won back in 1982 under its former title of the European Cup.

BUKAYO SAKA & MIKEL ARTETA

ARSENAL

GROUND: Emirates Stadium **CAPACITY:** 60,704
MANAGER: Mikel Arteta **NICKNAME:** The Gunners
2023/24 LEAGUE POSITION: Runners-up

DID YOU KNOW:
Arsenal have been Premier League runners-up on eight occasions.

BRENTFORD

GROUND: Gtech Community Stadium **CAPACITY:** 17,250
MANAGER: Thomas Frank **NICKNAME:** The Bees
2023/24 LEAGUE POSITION: 16th

DID YOU KNOW:
When the Bees won promotion to the Premier League in 2021, it ended the club's 74-year top flight absence.

BRIGHTON & HOVE ALBION

GROUND: The Amex Stadium **CAPACITY:** 31,780
MANAGER: Fabian Hürzeler **NICKNAME:** The Seagulls
2023/24 LEAGUE POSITION: 11th

DID YOU KNOW:
Aged just 31, Albion's Fabian Hürzeler is the youngest head coach in the Premier League.

EVERTON

GROUND: Goodison Park **CAPACITY:** 39,414
MANAGER: Sean Dyche **NICKNAME:** The Toffees
2023/24 LEAGUE POSITION: 15th

DID YOU KNOW:
Goodison Park has been home to Everton since 1892, but in 2025 the club are set to take-up residence at their new ground on Bramley-Moore Dock.

CHELSEA

GROUND: Stamford Bridge **CAPACITY:** 40,323
MANAGER: Enzo Maresca **NICKNAME:** The Blues
2023/24 LEAGUE POSITION: 6th

DID YOU KNOW:
Chelsea remain the only London club to win the UEFA Champions League, in 2012 and above in 2021.

FULHAM

GROUND: Craven Cottage **CAPACITY:** 29,600
MANAGER: Marco Silva **NICKNAME:** The Whites
2023/24 LEAGUE POSITION: 13th

DID YOU KNOW:
Two former England managers Kevin Keegan and Roy Hodgson have both also managed Fulham.

EBERECHI EZE IN EURO 24 ACTION

CRYSTAL PALACE

GROUND: Selhurst Park **CAPACITY:** 25,486
MANAGER: Oliver Glasner **NICKNAME:** The Eagles
2023/24 LEAGUE POSITION: 10th

DID YOU KNOW:
No club had more players in England's Euro 24 squad than Palace's four - Eberechi Eze, Marc Guéhi, Dean Henderson and Adam Wharton.

IPSWICH TOWN

GROUND: Portman Road **CAPACITY:** 29,673
MANAGER: Kieran McKenna **NICKNAME:** Tractor Boys
2023/24 LEAGUE POSITION: 2nd Championship

DID YOU KNOW:
The 2024/25 season sees Town competing in the Premier League for the first time since 2002.

It's time to get to grips with the Premier League and...

MEET YOUR RIVALS

MANCHESTER CITY

GROUND: Etihad Stadium **CAPACITY:** 53,400
MANAGER: Pep Guardiola **NICKNAME:** The Citizens
2023/24 LEAGUE POSITION: Champions

DID YOU KNOW:
Last season's title triumph saw Manchester City become the first team to win four consecutive Premier League titles.

LIVERPOOL

GROUND: Anfield **CAPACITY:** 62,276
MANAGER: Arne Slot **NICKNAME:** The Reds
2023/24 LEAGUE POSITION: 3rd

DID YOU KNOW:
New Reds' boss Arne Slot is the first Dutchman to manage the Merseyside giants.

MANCHESTER UNITED

BRUNO FERNANDES & ERIK TEN HAG

GROUND: Old Trafford **CAPACITY:** 74,140
MANAGER: Erik ten Hag **NICKNAME:** The Red Devils
2023/24 LEAGUE POSITION: 8th

DID YOU KNOW:
Manchester United have competed in the top division of English football in every season since 1975.

NEWCASTLE UNITED

GROUND: St James' Park **CAPACITY:** 52,305
MANAGER: Eddie Howe **NICKNAME:** The Magpies
2023/24 LEAGUE POSITION: 7th

DID YOU KNOW:
With 260 Premier League goals, Match of the Day pundit and former Newcastle striker Alan Shearer holds the Premier League's top marksman record.

TOTTENHAM HOTSPUR

GROUND: Tottenham Hotspur Stadium
CAPACITY: 62,850
MANAGER: Ange Postecoglou **NICKNAME:** Spurs
2023/24 LEAGUE POSITION: 5th

DID YOU KNOW:
Tottenham Hotspur made Wembley their home ground for fixtures when White Hart Lane was being transformed to the new Tottenham Hotspur Stadium.

NOTTINGHAM FOREST

GROUND: The City Ground **CAPACITY:** 30,332
MANAGER: Nuno Espírito Santo **NICKNAME:** Forest
2023/24 LEAGUE POSITION: 17th

DID YOU KNOW:
Nottingham Forest were back-to-back European Cup winners in 1978/79 and 1979/80.

WEST HAM UNITED

GROUND: London Stadium **CAPACITY:** 62,500
MANAGER: Julen Lopetegui **NICKNAME:** The Hammers
2023/24 LEAGUE POSITION: 9th

DID YOU KNOW:
In 2023 West Ham United became the first English team to win the UEFA Europa Conference League.

SOUTHAMPTON

GROUND: St Mary's Stadium **CAPACITY:** 32,384
MANAGER: Russell Martin **NICKNAME:** The Saints
2023/24 LEAGUE POSITION: 4th Championship

DID YOU KNOW:
Last season's promotion via the Play-Offs was the first time the Saints have bounced back to the top division at the first attempt following relegation.

WOLVES

GROUND: Molineux **CAPACITY:** 32,050
MANAGER: Gary O'Neil **NICKNAME:** Wolves
2023/24 LEAGUE POSITION: 14th

DID YOU KNOW:
Since the 1986/87 season Wolverhampton Wanderers have competed in all four divisions of the English football pyramid.

LCFC Women are fast establishing themselves as a Barclays Women's Super League side, finishing 10th in their third season in the top flight, achieving new records in the form of a highest-ever points tally and most goals scored while conceding fewer.

LCFC WOMEN

The 2023/24 season started off in stunning fashion, winning 4-2 away from home against Bristol City, in which three debutants got on the scoresheet, and went unbeaten in their first four games in October.

Throughout a long and testing season, which included beating Manchester City on penalties and having a trip to Emirates Stadium, their proudest moments came in the Adobe Women's FA Cup.

Beating Derby County and Birmingham City in their first two games of the competition, the Foxes headed to Prenton Park to face Liverpool in the Quarter-Finals. Top goalscorer Jutta Rantala found the net twice to send Leicester through to the final four for their first time in history.

Arriving with nearly 2,000 Leicester fans in tow, City took an early lead through Rantala at Tottenham Hotspur Stadium, but unfortunately fell short in extra-time. However, the incredible run in the FA Cup will still live long in the memory.

In a first season since LCFC Women's Academy gained their Tier 1 Pro Game Status, the next line of recruits came through the ranks at Belvoir Drive; one of which, young striker Denny Draper, quickly caught attention, becoming the Club's youngest ever goalscorer, netting in a 5-2 win over the Robins at King Power Stadium.

Now preparing for a fourth consecutive season at the top level of English football, Amandine Miquel has taken charge of the Foxes, and arrives from French side Stade De Reims, alongside Assistant Manager Amaury Messuwe and forward Noémie Mouchon.

The squad has also been bolstered with the additions of Jamaican international Chantelle Swaby and Belgian defender Sari Kees, with a permanent return to Filbert Way for talented midfielder Ruby Mace.

With every Leicester WSL game confirmed at King Power Stadium, make sure to get yourself down and support Amandine's squad as they aim for new heights and look to continue making history.

LCFC WOMEN SQUAD 24/25

COURTNEY NEVIN — 2
POSITION: Defender **COUNTRY:** Australia **DOB:** 12/02/2002

An initial loan spell for young full-back Nevin saw her register five assists in the second half of 2022/23 before penning a permanent deal, with previous experience at Western Sydney Wanderers and Hammarby IF.

JANINA LEITZIG — 1
POSITION: Goalkeeper **COUNTRY:** Germany **DOB:** 16/04/1999

Leitzig joined the Foxes on loan from Bayern Munich during the 2022/23 campaign, and quickly captured the hearts of the Foxes faithful, ensuring a permanent move to Filbert Way the following year where she made 18 appearances in all competitions.

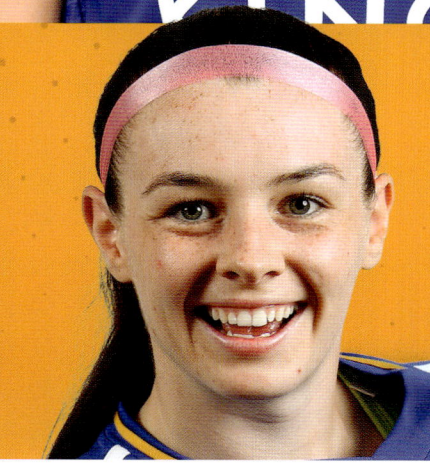

SAM TIERNEY — 3
POSITION: Midfielder **COUNTRY:** England **DOB:** 08/10/1998

Sheffield-born Tierney became the first LCFC Women player to hit 100 appearances and remains the all-time top appearance maker. A versatile individual who has played from centre-half to attacking midfield, she was part of the Barclays Women's Championship title-winning side.

CJ BOTT — 4
POSITION: Defender **COUNTRY:** New Zealand **DOB:** 22/04/1995

CJ joined the Foxes before their second season in the WSL and brought a wealth of experience from her homeland, Germany and Sweden before her footballing journey brought her to the East Midlands, where she has played 51 times and most recently featured for the Ferns at the Paris 2024 Olympics.

SAORI TAKARADA — 6
POSITION: Midfielder **COUNTRY:** Japan **DOB:** 27/12/1999

A talented holding midfielder that excels at breaking up play, Takarada came to City during the winter transfer window after two successful seasons with Linköpings FC in Sweden's top flight. With five goal involvements already, there is much excitement around her upcoming first full campaign at the Club.

SOPHIE HOWARD — 5
POSITION: Defender **COUNTRY:** Scotland **DOB:** 17/08/1993

The second LCFC Women player to make 100 appearances, the ever-present centre-back also has 50 caps for Scotland. Scoring five goals during her time in Leicestershire, City's No.5 has become part of the furniture at the Foxes.

DEANNE ROSE — 7
POSITION: Forward **COUNTRY:** Canada **DOB:** 03/03/1998

Providing an injection of pace on the football pitch, Rose signed for the Foxes on a two-year deal ahead of the 2023/24 campaign, and scored three goals in her first season, including two in during a historic Adobe Women's FA Cup campaign.

LCFC WOMEN SQUAD 24/25

JUTTA RANTALA — 8
POSITION: Forward **COUNTRY:** Finland **DOB:** 11/11/1999

Finland forward Rantala joined the Foxes from Vittsjö GIK and scored a brace on her debut against Bristol City before going on to hit double figures in all competitions during the 2023/24 season - the first Foxes player to do so since becoming a WSL team.

NOÉMIE MOUCHON — 10
POSITION: Forward **COUNTRY:** France **DOB:** 06/06/2003

French attacker Mouchon completed a move to Leicestershire following a successful spell in the Première Ligue with Stade De Reims last term, finishing fourth and a return of nine goals in 22 league appearances under the guidance of Amandine Miquel.

LENA PETERMANN — 9
POSITION: Forward **COUNTRY:** Germany **DOB:** 05/02/1994

The experienced striker spent four years with French Montpellier before moving across to England. City's number nine scored six goals in her debut campaign, including a Goal of the Season contender against Brighton & Hove Albion.

JANICE CAYMAN — 11
POSITION: Midfielder **COUNTRY:** Belgium **DOB:** 12/10/1988

A two-time UEFA Women's Champions League winner with Olympique Lyonnais, Cayman made the switch to Belvoir Drive ahead of the 2023/24 season, scoring seven times in 29 games, and is preparing for her second WSL term with the Club at the age of 35.

ASMITA ALE — 12
POSITION: Defender   COUNTRY: England   DOB: 03/11/2001

Spending the second half of 2023/24 on loan at Leicester from Tottenham Hotspur, the England Under-23s international full-back made eight appearances before completing a permanent summer move under Amandine Miquel's management.

EMILIA PELGANDER — 18
POSITION: Midfielder   COUNTRY: Sweden   DOB: 03/03/2004

An exciting talent from Sweden, Pelgander signed a long-term deal during the 2023/24 season, arriving from KIF Örebro and made her debut against Manchester City in the WSL in February.

JULIE THIBAUD — 17
POSITION: Defender   COUNTRY: France   DOB: 20/04/1998

An accomplished ball-playing defender, Thibaud's move to Leicester was her first outside of her home nation and she went on to make 26 appearances in a solid debut season at centre-back.

DENNY DRAPER — 19
POSITION: Forward   COUNTRY: England   DOB: 17/03/2007

Academy graduate Draper signed her first professional deal in the summer of 2024 and looks forward to her first full season in the First Team, where she has already made four appearances, becoming the youngest ever goalscorer when she found the net in a 5-2 win over Bristol City.

MISSY GOODWIN — 20
POSITION: Forward **COUNTRY:** England **DOB:** 27/01/2003

Signed in January 2022, Goodwin has made over 50 appearances for Leicester following her Midlands switch from Aston Villa, claiming the 2023/24 Goal of the Season award with a phenomenal left-footed effort against Liverpool at Prenton Park.

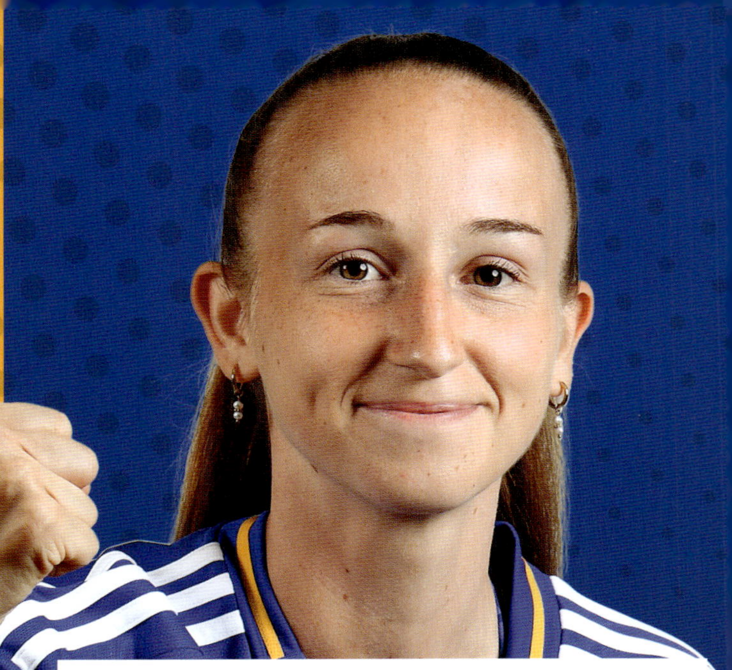

SARI KEES — 22
POSITION: Defender **COUNTRY:** Belgium **DOB:** 17/02/2001

Signed from Belgian side OH Leuven on a three-year deal, the 23-year-old arrived having represented Belgium 30 times on the international stage. Already a member of the King Power football family, the exciting defender joins for the 2024/25 WSL season.

HANNAH CAIN — 21
POSITION: Forward **COUNTRY:** Wales **DOB:** 11/02/1999

A Welsh international, Cain has played 45 times for the Foxes since joining in the summer of 2020. Part of the Championship-winning side, the forward is currently recovering from her second ACL injury.

LIZE KOP — 23
POSITION: Goalkeeper **COUNTRY:** Netherlands **DOB:** 17/03/1998

Arriving from Ajax, Kop challenged Janina Leitzig for the goalkeeper spot, playing in each FA Cup game, all the way through to the Semi-Final in London against Tottenham.

LCFC WOMEN SQUAD 24/25

SHANNON O'BRIEN — 27
POSITION: Forward **COUNTRY:** England **DOB:** 05/10/2001

Another Aston Villa graduate that made the move to Leicester, O'Brien played her part in City's promotion to the Super League, opening her account in March 2021 with a brace against London Bees and recently signed a new long-term contract.

RUBY MACE — 30
POSITION: Midfielder **COUNTRY:** England **DOB:** 05/09/2003

Signing a two-year contract, the highly-rated youngster primarily operates in the middle of the park and rejoins the Foxes on a permanent basis after impressing during a loan spell in the 2022/23 campaign, where she made 11 appearances.

YUKA MOMIKI — 29
POSITION: Forward **COUNTRY:** Japan **DOB:** 09/04/1996

A magician on the field, New York born Momiki joined City during the 2023/24 season from Linköping FC in Sweden, and made an immediate impression, scoring twice and assisting six goals.

CHANTELLE SWABY — 31
POSITION: Defender **COUNTRY:** Jamaica **DOB:** 06/08/1998

Born in Connecticut, USA, the 25-year-old joined the Foxes following her departure from FC Fleury 91 in France's top division and has competed in both the World Cup and CONCACAF championships since debuting for Jamaica in 2018.

WORD SEARCH

WORDS CAN GO IN ANY DIRECTION, EVEN DIAGONALS, AND CAN OVERLAP EACH OTHER.

ALL OF THE PREMIER LEAGUE CLUBS' NICKNAMES ARE HIDDEN IN THE GRID, EXCEPT FOR ONE …BUT CAN YOU WORK OUT WHICH ONE?

ANSWERS ON PAGE 62

```
Y S N A L L I V C D S L I V E D D E R S
H P I O M C Q T M B W I M P C Z H L B F
O Z E B Q T R U Q P E J J Z P I Q S E
S O Z A M Q Z X T N B E M A G P I E S H
I J V T G C H B R O W I S V D O R T T E
Y H K T L L V S A C D R S U S L J U W D
C M H O I F E M C S H E D R O H B L V Q
Q S W R E S T N W E U X K P L V W G
Y Y E W X O O I O E Z P R M B E U C H W
L D O V F X P S R Z S V J R F U E O I X
S I D F L D G Z B I J B Y Y I O S H T Q
C J E P W O O L O T P S Y F F E R Z E E
A E Y F V D W F Y I A E F W E Z S E S W
S U H C L J S B S C S X D P Q E K F S J
P P T Y A B U A U U O O T U A J R C Z T
G H W U S V O C I D F F X G T S A P B J
G H R N Q S R E N N U G U P S H R X G R
B M Q D V B K Z A I T L I A Z S W X R B
C S B U K L B E R D L S X R T Q W I M J
F Y F G X C T D I S R J J E S B X V E Z
```

BEES	FOREST	RED DEVILS	TOFFEES
BLUES	FOXES	REDS	TRACTOR BOYS
CHERRIES	GUNNERS	SAINTS	VILLANS
CITIZENS	HAMMERS	SEAGULLS	WHITES
EAGLES	MAGPIES	SPURS	WOLVES

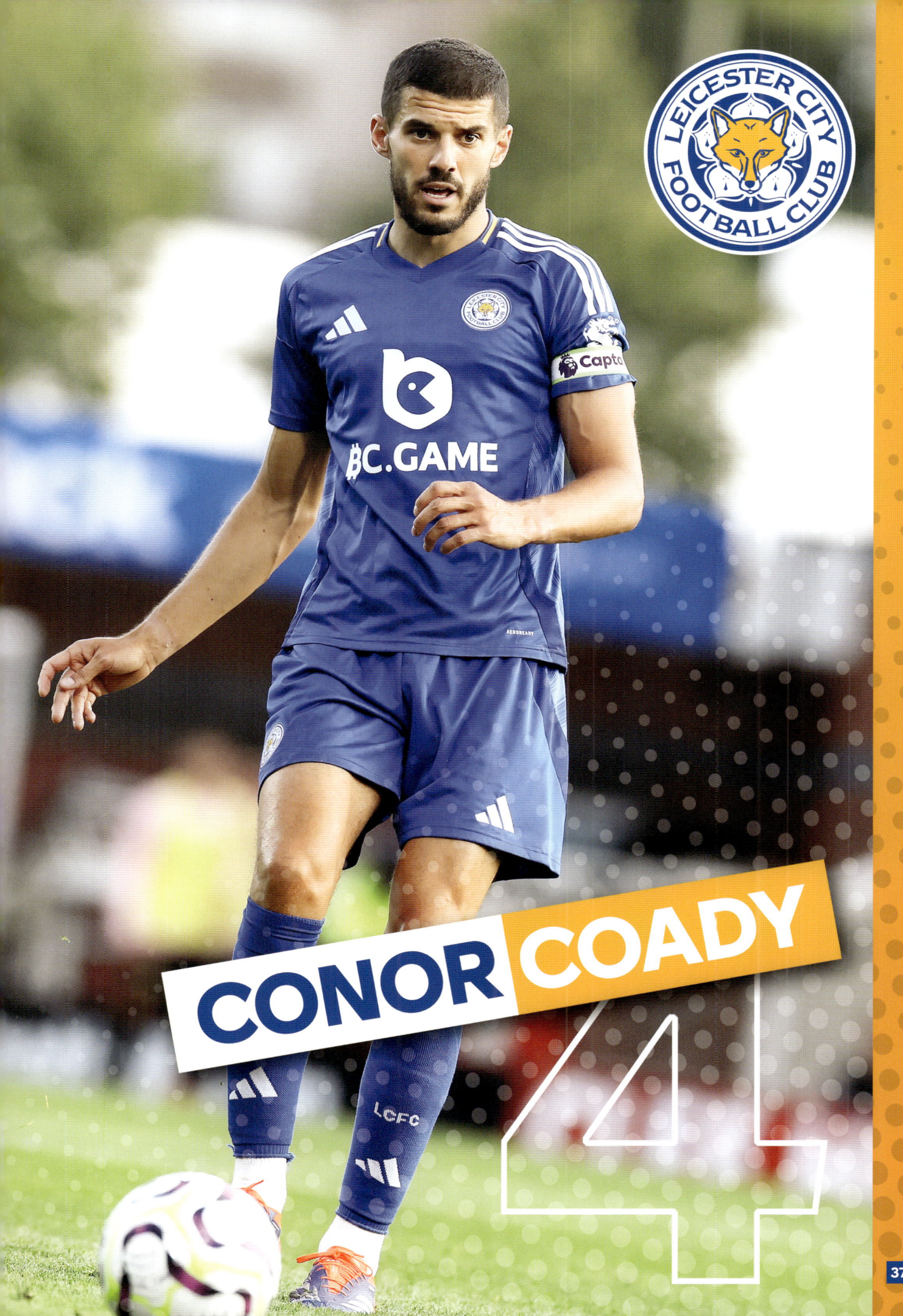

BIG MATCH

Can you match each of these players to the number of goals they scored for the Foxes?

ANSWERS ON PAGE 62

A. PLAYER: GOALS:

B. PLAYER: GOALS:

C. PLAYER: GOALS:

D. PLAYER: GOALS:

E. PLAYER: GOALS:

F. PLAYER: GOALS:

G. PLAYER: GOALS:

H. PLAYER: GOALS:

ARTHUR CHANDLER · GEORGE DEWIS · ERNIE HINE · DEREK HINES · GARY LINEKER · ARTHUR LOCHHEAD · ARTHUR ROWLEY · JAMIE VARDY

273 · 265 · 190 · 156 · 117 · 114 · 113 · 103

Watch out for these danger men when City meet their Premier League rivals...

DANGER MEN

AFC BOURNEMOUTH
Antoine Semenyo

Ghanaian international forward Antoine Semenyo offers Cherries' boss Andoni Iraola several options in attack with the pacy 24-year-old able to play as a winger or as a central striker.

Signed from Bristol City in January 2023 for £10M, Semenyo is a tricky customer whose close control skills and speed make him a defender's nightmare. He weighed in with eight Premier League goals last season and began the new 2024/25 season in fine form when he netted the Cherries' opening-day equaliser at Nottingham Forest.

ASTON VILLA
Ollie Watkins

Having scored England's dramatic UEFA Euro 2024 semi-final winner against the Netherlands, Aston Villa striker Ollie Watkins is sure to start the 2024/25 season brimming with confidence.

Watkins' heroics with the Three Lions came after the 28-year-old forward had enjoyed a sensational season at club level with Unai Emery's team.

The former Brentford man netted a superb 19 Premier League goals in Villa colours in 2023/24 as the club secured UEFA Champions League football for 2024/25.

ARSENAL
Bukayo Saka

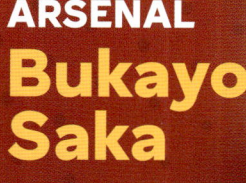

A star performer for club and country, England's Bukayo Saka is sure to once again play a pivotal part in Arsenal's latest bid for Premier League glory.

Operating on the right side of the Gunners' attack, Saka can cut inside and unleash efforts on goal himself or pick out team-mates with the perfect through ball.

Saka topped the Gunners' Premier League scoring charts last season with 16 goals from 35 appearances as Arsenal finished runners-up.

BRENTFORD
Yoane Wissa

A fast and sharp forward with an eye for goal, 28-year-old Yoane Wissa netted a dozen times in Brentford's 2023/24 Premier League campaign, including strikes in consecutive London derbies against West Ham Utd, Chelsea and Arsenal.

Signed from Lorient in 2021, Wissa has now made over a century of appearances for Brentford and his ability to function in several attacking roles for Thomas Frank's side has seen him emerge as a great asset to the Bees.

BRIGHTON & HOVE ALBION
Danny Welbeck

A player who just appears to get better with age, 33-year-old Danny Welbeck has certainly proved to be a shrewd signing for the Seagulls.

The former Manchester United and Arsenal forward contributed five goals to Albion's 2023/24 Premier League campaign. His strength, experience and his ability to hold the ball, bring team-mates into play and finish opportunities are sure to make him one of the first names on the Albion teamsheet again in 2024/25.

EVERTON
Jordan Pickford

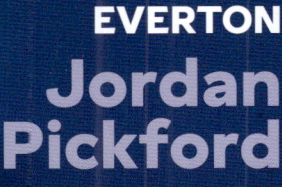

England's undisputed first choice goalkeeper, Jordan Pickford provides the last line of defence for Premier League Everton.

An outstanding goalkeeper who has played a crucial role in Everton's recent battles to secure Premier League status. Pickford's presence certainly adds a great deal of confidence to any defensive unit operating in front of him. Blessed with exceptional reflexes and comfortable with the ball at his feet, Pickford commands his area as well as any 'keeper in the world.

CHELSEA
Cole Palmer

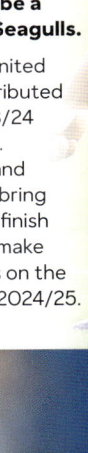

Chelsea supporters will just be hopeful of seeing more of the same from forward Cole Palmer who ended his debut season at Stamford Bridge with a superb 25-goal haul in all competitions.

In a tricky season for Chelsea, Cole was the club's big bright spot following his £40m switch from Manchester City in September 2023. A hat-trick hero for Chelsea in a thrilling 4-3 victory over Manchester United in April 2024, Cole was a member of England's Euro 2024 squad and was on target in the final against Spain.

FULHAM
Rodrigo Muniz

Exciting Brazilian striker Rodrigo Muniz gave the Fulham fans a true demonstration of his attacking prowess with 10 Premier League goals in the final four months of the 2023/24 season.

Great things are expected of the 23-year-old who would appear to be the man set to lead the Whites' attack in 2024/25.

Muniz has the natural talent to score memorable goals and the knack of being in the right place at the right in and around the penalty area too.

CRYSTAL PALACE
Adam Wharton

Midfielder Adam Wharton enjoyed a meteoric rise to fame in 2024 as he emerged to be a polished Premier League performer with Crystal Palace.

After agreeing a switch from Blackburn Rovers to Selhurst Park in February, Wharton had no difficulty in stepping up from the Championship to the Premier League and after just 16 Premier League games, Wharton was rewarded with his England debut against Bosnia and Herzegovina in June.

IPSWICH TOWN
Omari Hutchinson

Attacking wide-man Omari Hutchinson converted his loan move from Chelsea to Ipswich Town into a permanent arrangement in the summer of 2024 after proving a great success while on loan at Portman Road.

The 20-year-old netted 10 goals in Town's surprise promotion from the Championship and will now be looking to showcase his tricky wing play on the Premier League scene. Ipswich Town parted with a club record £20M to secure his talent on a permanent basis.

Watch out for these danger men when City meet their Premier League rivals...

Danger Men

MANCHESTER CITY

Erling Haaland

With an incredible 63 goals in 66 Premier League games in his first two seasons at the Etihad Stadium, Norwegian goal machine Erling Haaland leads the champions attack with supreme goalscoring efficiency.

With a further 27 goals in other competitions for all-conquering Manchester City, the 2024/25 season appears set to see Haaland hit the century-mark in City colours.

Unsurprisingly, Haaland has won the Premier League Golden Boot award, as the division's top scorer, in both 2022/23 and 2023/24.

LIVERPOOL

Cody Gakpo

Liverpool's Netherlands international striker Cody Gakpo is another Premier League star who performed well at the UEFA Euro 2024 finals in Germany.

Gakpo featured in six games for the Netherlands, netting three goals and registering one assist as his country reached the semi-final stage. Blessed with raw pace and an ability to get shots away early, all at Anfield will be hopeful of seeing the 25-year-old at his very best under new manager Arne Slot in 2024/25.

MANCHESTER UNITED

Kobbie Mainoo

Teenage sensation Kobbie Mainoo enjoyed a breakthrough season at Old Trafford in 2023/24 and his club form subsequently won him a place in England's squad for the UEFA Euro 2024 finals.

Despite his tender years, Mainoo is already recognised as a starter for both Manchester United and England. Blessed with great skill on the ball, the teenager's ability to carry the ball forward and help turn defence into attack makes him an extremely exciting talent.

NEWCASTLE UNITED
Harvey Barnes

Newcastle United fans will be hoping that England international Harvey Barnes enjoys an injury-free 2024/25 season at St James' Park.

The talented winger saw his debut campaign with the Magpies interrupted by an injury which sidelined him from September 2023 to February 2024. However, when he was fit and available, he was in tremendous form and netted five goals for Eddie Howe's team who certainly carried a greater attacking threat with Barnes in the side.

TOTTENHAM HOTSPUR
James Maddison

A surprise omission from the Three Lions' UEFA Euro 2024 finals squad, Spurs midfielder James Maddison is sure to have a point to prove during the 2024/25 season.

Maddison was an impressive performer in his debut campaign at Tottenham Hotspur Stadium despite missing a chunk of the season with an injury. The creative force in Spurs' midfield, Maddison netted four goals in 2023/24 while creating countless opportunities with his intelligent approach play.

NOTTINGHAM FOREST
Morgan Gibbs-White

Blessed with strength, speed, and clever close control, Nottingham Forest's Morgan Gibbs-White can break the lines and swiftly turn defence into attack.

A great creator of chances for others, he is one of the first names on head coach Nuno Espírito Santo's teamsheet. Gibbs-White was signed from Premier League rivals Wolverhampton Wanderers in August 2022 and with 10 goals in his first two seasons from midfield, the 24-year-old has been a roaring success at the City Ground.

WEST HAM UNITED
Jarrod Bowen

A real live wire performer in the Hammers' attack, Jarrod Bowen cemented his place in the West Ham United history books when he bagged the winning goal in the 2022/23 UEFA Europa Conference League Final.

Joining the Hammers in 2020 from Hull City, his speed, energy and style of play have made him a firm fans' favourite. With the flexibility to operate in various attacking positions, Bowen netted 20 goals last season and was part of England's Euro 2024 squad.

SOUTHAMPTON
Adam Armstrong

Adam Armstrong's goals proved vital in the Saints' instant return to the Premier League as 2023/24 Play-Off winners.

Armstrong bagged 21 league goals for Russell Martin's team before then adding another three to his tally in the Play-Offs, including the Wembley winner against Leeds United. Saints' fans will now be looking for Armstrong to bring his scoring boots to the Premier League in 2024/25.

WOLVES
Hwang Hee-chan

South Korean international striker Hwang Hee-chan had his best season to date in Wolves' colours in 2023/24 having bagged a dozen Premier League goals for the Molineux club.

A hard-working striker whose performances have won him great popularity with the Wolves faithful, Hwang joined Wolves in the summer of 2021 on a season-long loan deal from RB Leipzig. After impressing in his opening months in the Premier League, Wolves made the deal a permanent one in January 2022.

YOUNG PLAYER OF THE SEASON 23/24

Winger Abdul Fatawu was named as Leicester City's Men's Young Player of the Season last term.

On loan from Sporting Lisbon, the Ghanaian quickly endeared himself to the Foxes faithful, before making his move permanent in the summer, signing a five-year contract.

Finding the net on seven occasions and registering 13 assists in 2023/24, including a magnificent hat-trick and assist for Jamie Vardy's goal in the crucial 5-0 victory over Southampton at King Power Stadium, he also set up Kasey McAteer in the 3-0 title-clinching success at Preston North End.

ABDUL

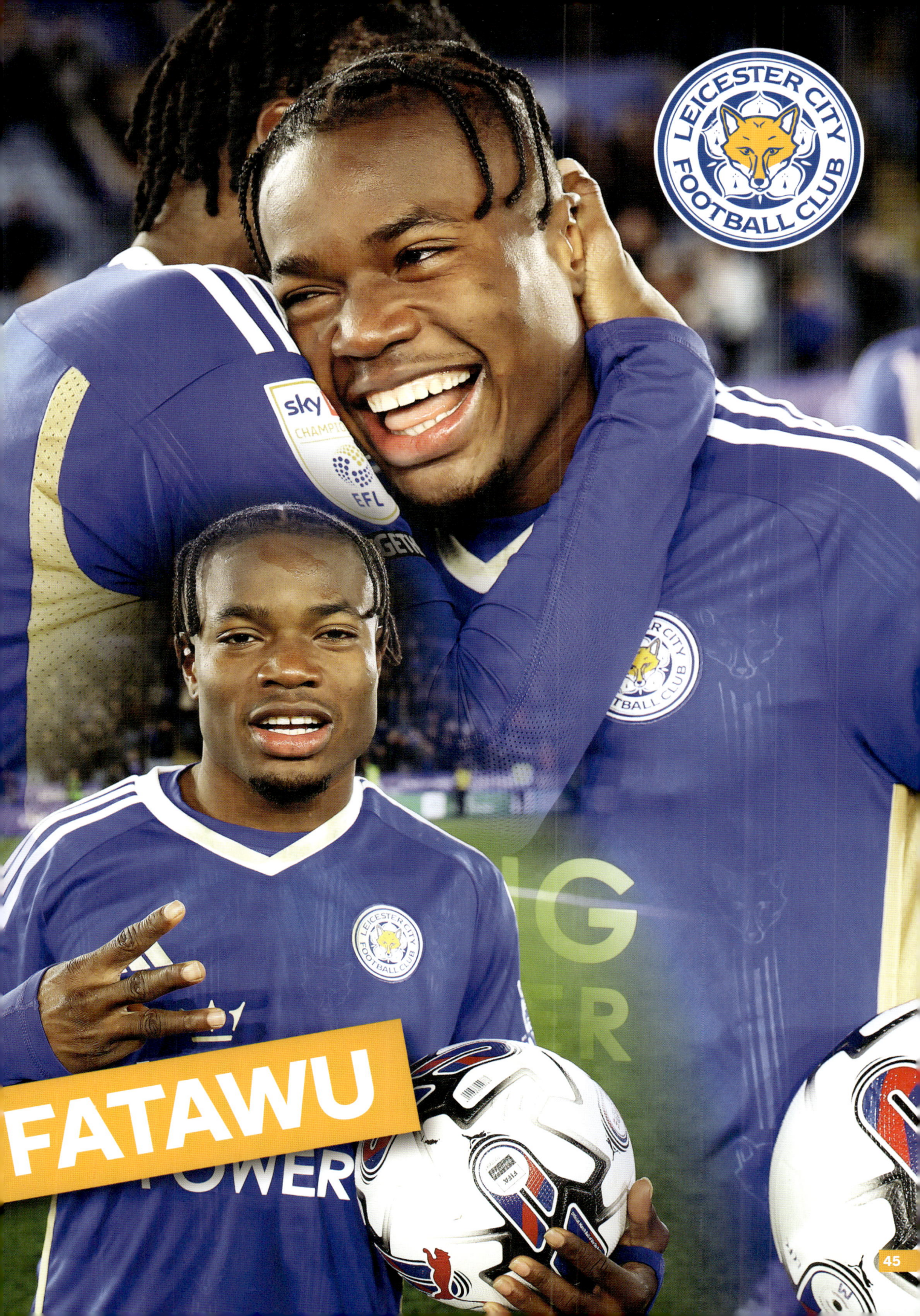

SET UP A SQUARE WITHIN SHOOTING DISTANCE OF YOUR GOAL. PLACE A KEEPER IN GOAL AND A DEFENDER INSIDE THE SQUARE. YOU AND THE REST OF YOUR MATES ARE ATTACKERS AND SHOULD START AT THE OTHER SIDE OF THE SQUARE FROM THE GOAL.

FOOTY DRILLS

ATTACK ATTACK

The purpose of this drill is to focus on dribbling to beat a defender and finishing with a shot on goal.

EASY

Dribble into the square, try to beat the defender and dribble out of the opposite side of the square. If you successfully dribble through the square without losing the ball, finish with a shot on goal! If you lose the ball to the defender or dribble out either side of the square, you must then switch places with the defender so that you are protecting the square and they become an attacker. The next player in line can go as soon as a shot on goal is taken or the defender has won the ball.

HARD

You can make the square bigger to make it easier for the attackers or make the square smaller to make it easier for the defenders.

EXPERT

You can make the square slightly larger and add a second defender so that the game becomes 2 v 1 and harder for the attacker. To make shooting harder, move the square further away from the goal and encourage a longer shot.

Remember to take turns being in goal so that everyone gets a chance to play all positions!

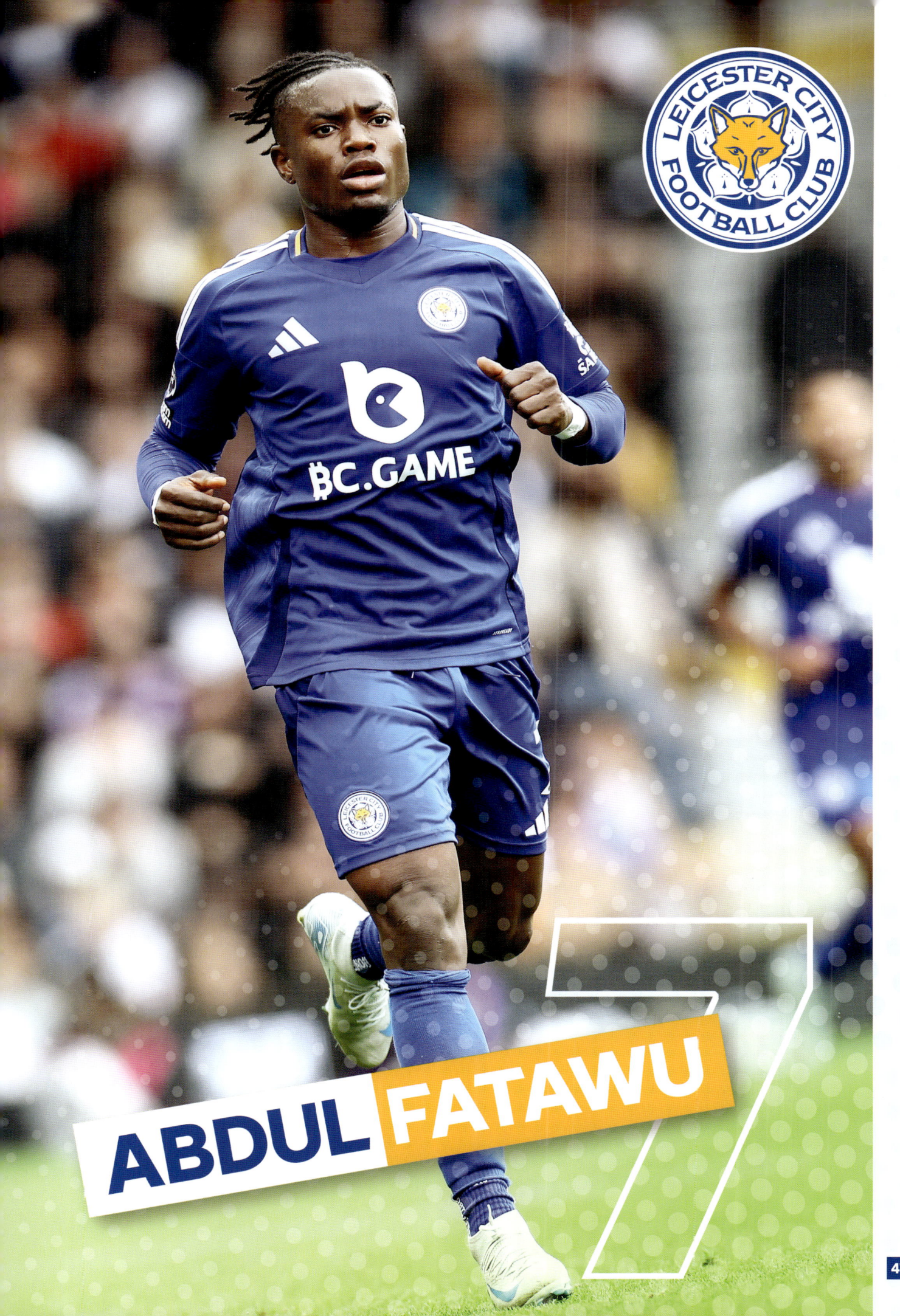

8 HARRY WINKS

LCFC WOMEN 23/24 PLAYER OF THE SEASON

Jutta Rantala romped home with both the LCFC Women Players' Player and Player of the Season awards for the 2023/24 campaign, hitting double figures for goals in her maiden WSL season with the Foxes.

Among those goals was an Adobe Women's FA Cup Semi-Final effort against Tottenham Hotspur. The Finnish forward took aim from outside the box and found the net in expert fashion. Despite the loss, it will live long in the memory of the Leicester fans in the capital that day.

Donning City's No.8 shirt since her arrival, it took no time for the Finland international to settle in, netting a brace on her debut against Bristol City at Ashton Gate, going on to score six times in the Barclays Women's Super League, registering seven assists across all competitions.

JUTTA RANTALA

With 17 goal involvements throughout the year, Rantala became a focal point of the attack, and formed on-field connections with her team-mates, including central striker Lena Petermann, who also enjoyed a promising debut campaign, finding the net on seven occasions.

A versatile forward who can play anywhere across the front line, the 24-year-old will have a big part to play on Filbert Way this coming campaign, as Amandine Miquel looks to develop Leicester into a top-half team.

The Young Player of the Season award went to Kiera Bell, who impressed in the backline for City's Under-21s Academy as they recorded a second-place finish in the PGA Under-21 League North Division, narrowly behind Manchester United.

Success did come in the cup competitions for the youngsters as they won the PGA Plate Final against Charlton Athletic and the County Cup against local side Anstey Nomads to round off the term.

In what was a testing first season since obtaining their Tier 1 Pro Game Status, City's Academy setup at Belvoir Drive aims to produce the next batch of WSL players in the East Midlands. Bell's recognised achievements last season are a perfect example of the Foxes' plans for the future.

MISSY GOODWIN

The 21-year-old has a good record against Liverpool, finding the net in April of last year when the two sides met at King Power Stadium. Goodwin's header, latching onto the end of a Courtney Nevin cross in added-time, rounded off a 4-0 scoreline in favour of Leicester - a club record WSL win which still stands to this day.

The former Aston Villa forward scored two goals throughout the duration of the 23/24 season, but her first of the campaign against Matt Beard's Liverpool was enough to claim the accolade at the awards evening on Filbert Way.

Signed in January 2022, Goodwin has gone on to make over 50 appearances for the Foxes as the former England Youth international looks to continue her development and will be hoping to make strides in the upcoming WSL campaign under Amandine Miquel.

The 2023/24 Goal of the Season award for LCFC Women went to Missy Goodwin for her spectacular effort against Liverpool at Prenton Park. Receiving the ball on the left wing, the talented English winger cut inside and fired a left-footed effort into the top corner of the Reds' net.

The match, all the way back in November of 2023, finished 2-1 in favour of the home club on Merseyside. Melissa Lawley opened the scoring before Goodwin's impressive equaliser with little under an hour on the clock in Tranmere.

A winner was found with less than 10 minutes to go through Marie Höbinger, as City slumped to what was only their second defeat of the season so far, after a rampant month of October which saw them go unbeaten in their first four matches.

23/24 GOAL OF THE SEASON

Here are 20 fun footy Fact or Fib teasers for you to tackle! Good luck...

FACT OR FIB?

01 The Foxes are set to face Liverpool at King Power Stadium in their final home game of the 2024/25 season.

02 Former Manchester United striker Ruud van Nistelrooy rejoined the Red Devils in the summer of 2024 as part of the coaching staff.

03 Arsenal have been Premier League runners-up in the past three seasons.

04 2024/25 campaign is due to be Everton's final campaign at Goodison Park.

05 Under the management of Martin O'Neill, Leicester City were League Cup winners in 1997 and 2000.

06 Of the 20 clubs competing in the 2024/25 Premier League only six have ever won the competition.

07 Jarrod Bowen was the only West Ham United player to make England's UEFA Euro 2024 squad.

08 The Tottenham Hotspur Stadium has the biggest capacity in the Premier League.

09 Leicester City's last trip to Wembley was for the 2021 Community Shield.

10 Manchester United have only once won the Premier League title since Sir Alex Ferguson left the club.

14 Premier League rivals Liverpool and Chelsea competed in the 2024 Carabao Cup Final.

11 Chelsea last won the Premier League title in 2017/18.

15 Liverpool's new Dutch manager Arne Slot was previously managing Ajax of Amsterdam.

18 Brentford's Gtech Community Stadium has the smallest capacity in the Premier League.

12 Wolverhampton Wanderers' head coach Gary O'Neil ended his playing career with a spell at Bolton Wanderers.

16 Manchester City's former home ground was called Maine Road.

19 Fulham head coach Marco Silva once managed West Bromwich Albion.

13 The Foxes signed club legend Jamie Vardy from Morecambe.

17 Foxes goalkeeper Mads Hermansen was ever-present in last season's Championship title triumph.

20 Aston Villa will be competing in the Champions League in 2024/25.

ANSWERS ON PAGE 62

SET UP THREE CONES IN A LARGE TRIANGLE. THESE BECOME OUR THREE GOALS!

MAKE SURE THE TRIANGLE IS BIG ENOUGH FOR THE GOALIE TO DIVE AROUND IN.

FOOTY DRILLS

SHOT STOPPING

The goalie stands in the centre of the triangle and three shooters stand opposite the three goals at their 'penalty spots'.

EASY

To start with, the shooters take it in turns to fire shots past the goalie. The goalie must work quickly to reposition himself for the next shot.

HARD

Players then start to fire shots more quickly. Just as the goalkeeper recovers from the last shot, the next player quickly shoots again.

EXPERT

Change the order in which the shooters take their shots. Shooters shout their names in any order, to signal that they are going to shoot. This keeps the goalie on his toes.

Also, be sure to try different shots. High, low, left foot, right foot, maybe even try chipping he ball over the keeper's head!

This drill is very tiring for the 'keeper. Remember to swap positions so that everyone gets the chance to be in goal.

GOAL OF THE SEASON 23/24

A superb long-range effort from Foxes full-back James Justin at Cardiff City in December was selected as the best strike of 2023/24 by the Blue Army at the Club's End of Season Awards.

The defender, who made 43 appearances in all competitions last term, explained his thinking for the goal, scored 10 minutes into the second half, which sealed a 2-0 win at Cardiff City Stadium for the table-toppers, after Kiernan Dewsbury-Hall opened the scoring in South Wales.

After claiming the accolade, Justin said: "It's something that I would never have expected at the start of the season, but to win the award - with all the special goals that we've scored this season - it means so much. For me to win the award, it's an amazing feeling.

"I think I took a touch to get it out my body and I looked at the goal. I thought: 'I'm not really sure about this one!' I decided to hit it and, in the end, it just went in and went in nicely."

Toasting the Club's eighth second-tier title was a moment to savour for Justin, who felt the achievement cannot be overstated.

JAMES JUSTIN

"It's been amazing celebrating it with all the fans and the team and the staff," Justin added. "It's been incredible. Promotion is not something that should be taken lightly. Especially going up as champions. It's something that we can all be proud of."

BIG MATCH

Can you match each of these players to the number of games they played for the Foxes?

ANSWERS ON PAGE 62

HUGH ADCOCK • ADAM BLACK • ARTHUR CHANDLER • GRAHAM CROSS • KASPER SCHMEICHEL • JAMIE VARDY • MARK WALLINGTON • STEVE WALSH

600 • 557 • 479 • 464 • 460 • 449 • 419

A. PLAYER: GAMES:

B. PLAYER: GAMES:

C. PLAYER: GAMES:

D. PLAYER: GAMES:

E. PLAYER: GAMES:

F. PLAYER: GAMES:

G. PLAYER: GAMES:

H. PLAYER: GAMES:

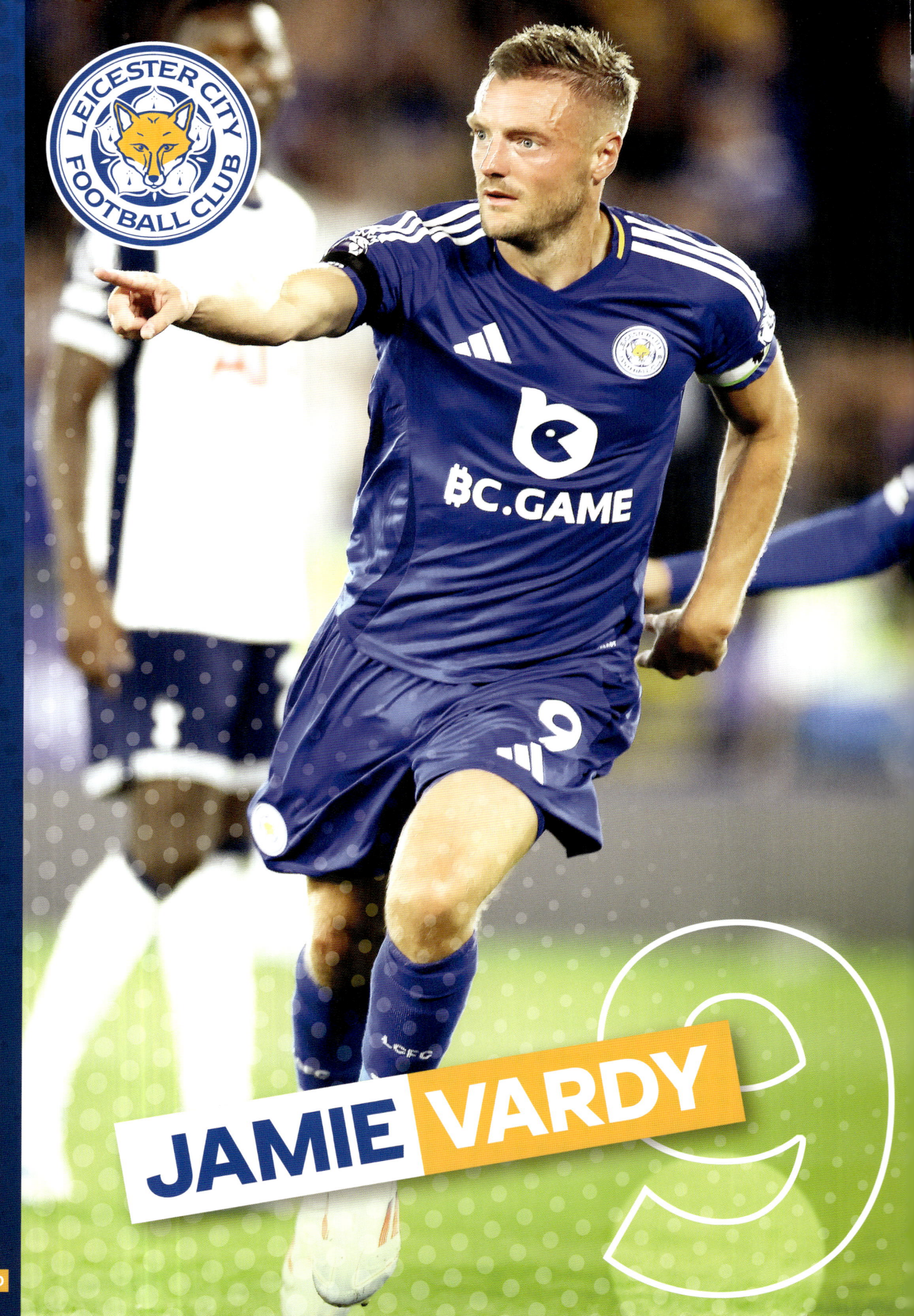

COMPLETE THE DRAWING OF THE CLUB BADGE

FOXES RULE

...and graffiti the wall with all things Leicester!

ANSWERS

PAGE 36 · WORDSEARCH

Hammers.

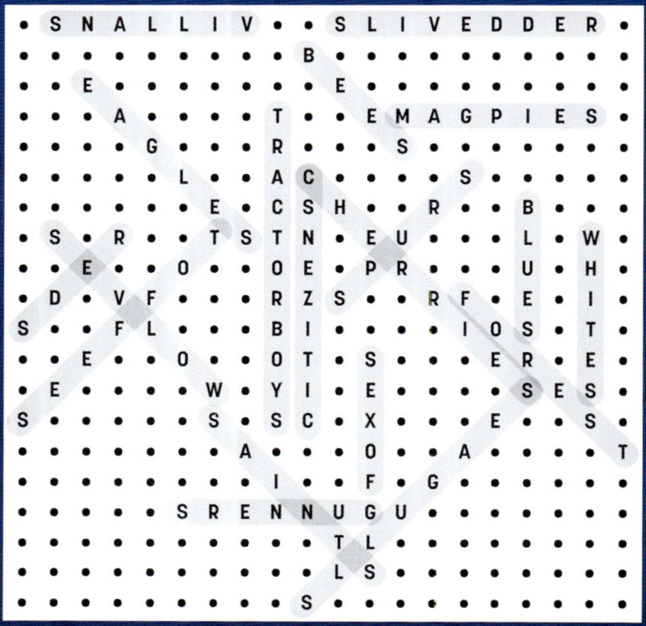

```
•  S  N  A  L  L  I  V  •  •  S  L  I  V  E  D  D  E  R
•  •  •  •  E  •  •  •  •  B  •  •  •  •  •  •  •  •
•  •  •  •  A  •  •  •  •  T  •  E  M  A  G  P  I  E  S
•  •  •  •  G  •  •  •  •  R  •  S  •  •  •  •  •  •
•  •  •  •  L  •  •  •  •  A  •  S  •  •  •  •  •  •
•  •  •  •  E  •  C  •  S  C  H  •  R  •  •  B  •  •
•  S  •  R  •  T  S  T  N  •  E  U  •  •  L  •  W
•  •  E  •  •  O  •  O  E  •  P  R  •  •  U  •  H
•  D  •  V  F  •  •  R  Z  S  •  •  R  F  •  E  •  I
•  S  •  F  L  •  •  •  B  I  •  •  I  O  •  •  •  T
•  •  E  •  O  •  •  •  O  T  •  •  S  •  •  E  •  E
•  E  •  •  W  •  •  •  Y  I  •  •  E  X  •  •  S  •  S
•  S  •  •  •  S  •  •  S  C  •  •  X  •  A  •  T
•  •  •  •  •  A  •  •  •  O  •  F  •  •  G  •  •
•  •  •  •  •  I  •  •  •  F  •  •  •  •  •  •  •
•  •  •  S  R  E  N  N  U  G  U  •  •  •  •  •  •
•  •  •  •  •  •  •  •  •  T  L  •  •  •  •  •  •
•  •  •  •  •  •  •  •  •  L  S  •  •  •  •  •  •
•  •  •  •  •  •  •  •  •  S  •  •  •  •  •  •  •
```

PAGE 38 · BIG MATCH - GOALS

A. Arthur Lochhead - 114. B. Derek Hines - 117.
C. Gary Lineker - 103. D. George Dewis - 113.
E. Jamie Vardy - 190. F. Ernie Hine - 156.
G. Arthur Chandler - 273. H. Arthur Rowley - 265.

PAGE 52 · FACT OR FIB?

1. Fib (They are due to host Ipswich Town in their final home game). 2. Fact. 3. Fib (Arsenal finished fifth in 2021/22). 4. Fact. 5. Fact. 6. Fact. 7. Fact. 8. Fib (Manchester United's Old Trafford has the biggest capacity in the Premier League). 9. Fact. 10. Fib (United have never won the title since Sir Alex Ferguson left). 11. Fib (Chelsea last won the title in 2016/17). 12. Fact. 13. Fib (Vardy was signed from Fleetwood). 14. Fact. 15. Fib (Slot was previously managing Feyenoord). 16. Fact. 17. Fib (He missed two league games). 18. Fib (AFC Bournemouth have the smallest capacity ground in the Premier League). 19. Fib (Silva has never managed West Bromwich Albion). 20. Fact.

PAGE 58 · BIG MATCH - GAMES

A. Hugh Adcock - 460. B. Mark Wallington - 460.
C. Arthur Chandler - 419. D. Steve Walsh - 449.
E. Adam Black - 557. F. Jamie Vardy - 464.
G. Graham Cross - 600. H. Kasper Schmeichel - 479.